DAY OF
DISASTER

BACKFIRE

VANESSA ACTON

MINNEAPOLIS

Darby Creek
A division of Lerner Publishing Group, Inc.
241 First Avenue North
Minneapolis, MN 55401 USA

For reading levels and more information, look up this title at
www.lernerbooks.com.

Front cover: © Tom Reichner/Shutterstock.com (fire), © iStockphoto.com/Marina Mariya (swirl).

Images in this book used with the permission of: © Tom Reichner/Shutterstock.com (fire), © iStockphoto.com/Marina Mariya (swirl).

Main body text set in Janson Text LT Std 12/17.5.
Typeface provided by Adobe Systems.

Library of Congress Cataloging-in-Publication Data

Names: Acton, Vanessa, author.
Title: Backfire / by Vanessa Acton.
Description: Minneapolis : Darby Creek, [2017] | Series: Day of disaster | Summary: "A wildfire threatens to obliterate everything in a boy's town. All he knows might be lost. Will he make it out in time? And will his home survive the blaze?"— Provided by publisher.
Identifiers: LCCN 2016019272 (print) | LCCN 2016034211 (ebook) | ISBN 9781512427752 (lb : alk. paper) | ISBN 9781512430943 (pb : alk. paper) | ISBN 9781512427820 (eb pdf)
Subjects: | CYAC: Wildfires—Fiction. | Fires—Fiction. | Survival—Fiction. | Nevada—Fiction.
Classification: LCC PZ7.1.A228 Bac 2017 (print) | LCC PZ7.1.A228 (ebook) | DDC [Fic]—dc23

LC record available at https://lccn.loc.gov/2016019272

Manufactured in the United States of America
1-41500-23361-7/21/2016

For H. A., who can't do simple math, and for
A. W., who can do so much more than that: I'll
need you on my team for the apocalypse.

Elijah

The day of the disaster, Elijah was bored out of his mind. He was supposed to be on a camping trip with his friends, not sitting at home with a dog who hated him and an uncle who treated him like a kid.

For the past forty-eight hours, Marco had kept Elijah busy with chores. "This is character building, Elijah"—Marco's favorite phrase. When your uncle is your legal guardian, you can still argue with him, but it won't get you very far.

This morning, Marco was giving Elijah a break. The lawn was mowed, the floors were mopped, the laundry was done. Elijah figured his character must be built enough for one weekend. Which meant he could spend today doing what Hayden, Nevada, was best known for: nothing.

So now Elijah sat on the living room couch watching *Storage Locker Makeover*. Serafina, the overweight dog, lay on the floor in front of the game cabinet with one suspicious eye open. That mutt must be at least half-cat. If you hugged her, petted her, even rubbed her ears, she'd look at you like, "Come on. Aren't we both adults?" After a year of living with Marco, Elijah had figured out that Serafina just wanted to be left alone. He respected that. He often felt the same way in Marco's house.

Elijah wondered when Brenna and Keegan and Nicole would get back from Topaz State Park. Probably tonight, since it was Sunday. School didn't start for three more weeks, but his friends all had summer jobs. He'd had one too, until this Thursday.

It hadn't been his fault, getting fired. He'd arranged for a coworker to cover his Thursday shift so he could pack for the trip. When the coworker didn't show up, the manager blamed Elijah. Never mind that people flaked on their shifts all the time—the manager had never liked Elijah. It had something to do with the fact that serving concessions in a movie theater wasn't Elijah's dream job. And the fact that Elijah got bored sometimes, messed around sometimes, ate patrons' leftover popcorn sometimes. In the manager's mind that added up to being a lazy, unreliable worker.

Elijah's uncle was on the manager's side. "You gave up on that job long before now," Marco had said. "You stopped trying. That's just as bad as if you'd quit." In Marco's mind, quitting was worse than some federal crimes. And even though Elijah hadn't *technically* quit, the punishment was the same.

Which was how a weekend of camping with friends became a weekend of "character building."

Elijah shifted on the couch. Like most of Marco's furniture, the couch was old. It had seen better times and fewer lumps. Elijah remembered sitting on it as a little kid, when Marco still lived in a trailer, years before he built this house.

The camping trip had been his idea in the first place—his and Brenna's. They had been friends since the sandbox stage of their lives, and both their families loved the outdoors. How many times had they all gone hiking or camping together at Topaz State Park? At least twice a year for as long as Elijah could remember. And now—with both Elijah's parents gone—he'd looked forward to this trip more than he liked to admit. Keegan would be there to crack jokes. Nicole would be there to get excited and amazed by every magical moment. And Brenna would be there to plan it all out, get them from Point A to Point B, and just let him be himself.

Instead, he was home, dealing with his un-built character. When the others got back, they'd tell him all their stories from the weekend. Nicole would say that they'd missed him, that it was a shame he couldn't come.

Keegan would ask, *What's your uncle's problem? Did he really have to ground you just because you lost your job? Doesn't he trust you at all?*

Elijah could only answer the third question: nope. Marco never trusted him. Maybe Marco thought Elijah's parents had rubbed off on him. Maybe Marco was just a jerk.

"THIS IS A SPECIAL BULLETIN FROM THE CONLEY COUNTY SHERRIFF'S OFFICE."

The voice on the TV cut off whatever the show's hosts had been saying. The screen now showed a local news anchor sitting behind a desk. "A wildfire is spreading rapidly through western Conley County," announced the newscaster. "High-speed winds are driving the flames north. A Level Three mandatory evacuation notice has been issued for the town of Carthage . . . "

Elijah sat up straight on the couch. Serafina lifted a floppy ear. Carthage was just to the south of Hayden. Wildfires weren't unusual this time of year, but Elijah couldn't remember the last time one had been this close.

The newscaster added, "The park service has evacuated one campsite in Topaz State Park. The rest of the park remains open. Park officials say that the fire is still not a threat to park facilities or visitors."

Topaz State Park. Elijah's thoughts went straight to his friends. *Are they in danger?*

The newscaster continued, "Level Two voluntary evacuation warnings are issued for Diamond Ridge, Hayden, and Scoria. Residents of these towns should be ready to leave their homes at a moment's notice."

Oh, crap. "Hey, Marco!" Elijah called

From the basement, his uncle responded, "Polo!"

And Elijah was the immature one, somehow.

"Get up here, man. There's a wildfire happening—and it's coming our way."

2

Brenna

All along, Brenna had had a bad feeling about this camping trip.

Partly because Elijah couldn't come. Brenna loved Keegan and Nicole, but they weren't experienced campers. Nicole had just moved to Hayden from Reno, and she'd never spent more than a few hours at a time outdoors. And Keegan had been to Topaz State Park only once, on an eighth grade field trip. Elijah, on the other hand, knew this whole area as well as Brenna did. They'd both camped and hiked here with their families every summer. Until last year, when Elijah's mom left and his dad went to prison.

If Elijah were here, this whole weekend would be going more smoothly, Brenna thought. Keegan wouldn't be questioning everything Brenna said. ("Are you sure that's the best route to Topaz Lake? Because I was thinking . . .") And Nicole would be trying a little harder. ("I mean, I *guess* we can go one more mile—if we *have* to.")

Elijah was good at convincing people. Brenna could make the exact same suggestion that Elijah would've made, say the exact same thing he would've said, and get crap for it. By now—the trip's third and final day—it had officially gotten on her nerves.

As the three of them hiked through the park on this hot Sunday morning, she kept reminding herself that normally Keegan and Nicole were great. Normally Nicole wasn't a complainer. Normally Keegan respected her intelligence. She loved them both—she really did—but she was never, ever going into the wilderness with them again.

It's more than that, though, Brenna thought. The uneasiness that'd been in her stomach all weekend wasn't just the result of her frustration. It wasn't just because they'd had to leave Elijah back in Hayden and the other two were getting under her skin.

So what else was bothering her?

The air.

It was so hot, so dry. Dangerously dry.

And if the air was dry, so was the ground: the grass, the brush, the aspen and juniper trees. Topaz State Park was one giant fire hazard.

It was peak wildfire season in Nevada. Every summer, the blazes seemed to be bigger and more frequent. Brenna's dad blamed careless people who set off fireworks or built bonfires in wooded areas. But the drought was the real problem. Without rain, all the vegetation was brittle. Everything burned more easily than usual. Once a fire started, it was harder to put out. The smallest spark could send a whole forest up in flames.

Brenna tried not to think about that. This was their last day at the park. They'd have to leave by early evening. *Quit stressing out and just enjoy yourself*, she thought, knowing that's what Elijah would tell her if he were here.

The three of them were heading uphill along the trail that led to Nero Canyon. Scrawny aspen trees surrounded them on either side. The hot sun filtered down through the branches. Brenna was already starting to sweat. She adjusted the bandanna wrapped around her forehead.

It felt good to be moving—and to know that she was carrying everything she needed. Her rolled-up sleeping bag and lightweight tent were strapped to the outside of her backpack. Inside the backpack she had her food, water, map, first aid kit, flashlight, compass, and phone. She'd had to save her money for a long time to afford her own gear. Everything she had was top-notch, but she didn't have anything beyond the essentials. None of the fancy extra gear that Keegan had brought—nylon rope, a mini-pickax and shovel, about six kinds of pocket knives . . .

"Hey, Bren." Keegan waved a hand in front of her face. "Are you sure it'll take us till noon to get to Nero Canyon?"

Brenna bit back a sigh. "Yep. It's simple math. Right now it's 10:15. We're about five miles away from the canyon. We just passed that sign that said so, remember? And we're walking at a speed of about three miles per hour—maybe a little slower since we're going uphill. So it'll take us a little less than two hours to reach the canyon."

"Okay, relax. I believe you."

"I *am* relaxed. I was just answering your question."

"Just a *yes* would've been fine."

Not true, though, thought Brenna. *Ever since we left Hayden, you've been testing me. It's like you can't trust my judgment unless I can prove I'm right.*

And she *could* prove it—because that was how her brain worked. Elijah always said that he loved the wilderness because it didn't have rules. But Brenna loved it for the opposite reason. Nature did have rules. It had shapes that broke down into perfect triangles, measurements that were all multiples of the same number. Nature was tricky and sometimes dangerous. But it did make sense.

Not like certain people. Not like Keegan, who was usually so laid-back. Brenna hadn't expected him to give her a hard time, to act like she was some kind of amateur. Being the only guy in the group and having a bunch of fancy equipment didn't make him the expert here.

"I wish we'd gone back to Topaz Lake instead," said Nicole. "I wanted to do some more swimming."

"You can swim at the community center," said Keegan. "Where in Hayden can you see a canyon? Plus there's a creek on the way."

"That's not the same," Nicole insisted. And what was wrong with *her*? Brenna had seen Nicole squeal with delight over a ladybug. Why wasn't Topaz State Park boggling her mind with its beauty? She had turned into a grumbler as mysteriously as Keegan had turned into a . . . Best not to finish that thought.

Being in the outdoors doesn't always bring out the best in people, Brenna reminded herself. *It probably isn't bringing out the best in me right now*

*either. I might be feeling less judgmental if I were
in an air-conditioned room.*

Keegan and Nicole kept debating the
merits of the canyon versus the lake. Brenna
stopped listening. If Elijah were here . . .

The wind suddenly shifted direction,
coming out of the southeast. It whipped at the
side of Brenna's face, as strong and warm as a
blow dryer.

The scent of burning leaves brushed
against her nose and trickled into her throat.
She paused, fiddling with her backpack strap.

"Do you smell that?" she asked the others.

"Oh my god," murmured Nicole. Brenna
took that as a yes.

"What?" said Keegan, sniffing doubtfully.

Brenna resisted the urge to roll her eyes
at him. He had to smell it. But she said it out
loud anyway.

"Smoke."

3

Elijah

Elijah could hear the TV from his bedroom. A news reporter was talking about firefighting methods.

"Firefighters are setting controlled backfires in the path of the fire's main front. These backfires will burn vegetation before the main fire reaches it, leaving the main fire with no fuel. If this strategy fails to slow the fire, the fire department will send in helicopters to spray water and fire retardant on the flames . . ."

Why are the controlled burns called backfires? Elijah wondered. *Not the most optimistic name.* Maybe he should ask his neighbor, Mrs. Lucas.

Her husband had been a firefighter.

"What are you doing?" Marco appeared in Elijah's bedroom doorway. He'd finally finished his morning workout and come upstairs.

Elijah looked up from the duffel bag he was packing. "Getting ready. In case we have to leave. Carthage just got evacuated. We might be next."

Marco squared his shoulders. He was a big-ish guy. Muscular. Even though he was only thirty, most people thought he was at least ten years older. He had the face of someone you wouldn't want to get in a fight with. "I'm not leaving this house. It's gonna take more than a little heat to send me running."

Marco was always saying dramatic stuff like this. He made a huge point of never giving up on anything, of finishing whatever he started. Elijah often wondered if Marco had been born this way—if his uncle and his dad had always been opposites. Or maybe Marco had become ultra-responsible on purpose to set himself apart from his brother.

Either way, it was irritating.

"This isn't just a little heat, Marco. It's miles and miles of fire. And it's, like, zero percent contained. The firefighters on the scene haven't made any progress at all. There's aerial footage on TV. It's not pretty."

"I won't let anything damage this house," said Marco grimly. "We'll fireproof the crap out of it. And I'll stand out there with a hose if I have to. Come on, let's get to work."

Elijah glanced at Serafina. The dog had gone back to napping—not that she would've taken Elijah's side.

I've clearly been grounded too long, Elijah thought. *I'm hoping a dog will back me up in an argument.*

Elijah spent the next half hour closing windows and doors, taking down curtains, moving furniture to the center of each room, and carrying the lawn chairs from the back patio to the basement. Meanwhile, Marco hooked up the garden hose outside and filled about six buckets with water.

"What are you doing, man?" asked Elijah as he joined him in the front yard. "Last time I checked, you weren't a firefighter."

"I'll fight anything that threatens my home," said Marco. "Get me a shovel and a rake from the garage, will you?"

"So you're gonna hold back the flames with a rake?"

"Just do it!"

Marco turned on the hose and aimed it at the side of the house. Elijah watched as the blast of water soaked the siding. Then he looked around at the rest of the front yard. Like most yards in the neighborhood, it was pretty bare: a sad-looking patch of freshly mowed brown grass, bordered by the driveway and the sidewalk. Marco had never planted bushes or trees. Landscaping wasn't his thing. Elijah, the incurable nature lover, had always thought it looked pretty depressing. But now it looked like a smartly maintained buffer zone—a protective barrier that would offer very little fuel for an oncoming wall of flame.

Elijah just wasn't sure it would be enough.

By now he could smell the smoke. There was a smudge of gray haze on the southern horizon. Hayden was a small town, built on flat land, with no tall buildings to block Elijah's view. So, on the upside, at least they'd be able to see the fire coming.

He headed for the garage. On his way, he pulled out his phone and tried calling Brenna. No luck. Cell service was pretty spotty at Topaz State Park, so that didn't surprise him. Still, he shot a group text to Brenna, Keegan, and Nicole, asking if they'd heard about the fire. Asking if they were okay. That was the best he could do right now.

In the garage, Elijah glanced at Marco's car. That would be their getaway vehicle if things got ugly and a mandatory evacuation went into effect. Marco had bought the car used, already on its last leg. When Elijah drove it, it stalled at least fifty percent of the time. He hoped it wouldn't pick today to die completely.

Elijah brought the rake to Marco, who immediately gave him another chore. "Go next door to check on Mrs. Lucas," Marco said. "See if she needs anything. Tell her I can hose down her house for her if she wants."

Mrs. Lucas was roughly two hundred years old. She was half-blind and half-deaf—maybe three-quarters deaf. But she worked in her vegetable garden every day. Did most of her own cooking and cleaning. Always managed to be flawlessly dressed. Elijah had once spotted her on her roof, cleaning the gutters. He was pretty sure that if she wanted the outside of her house sprayed with a hose, she could do it herself.

The one thing she couldn't do was drive.

***

"Oh, don't worry about me," chirped Mrs. Lucas when she finally answered the door. She was a tiny woman with skin the color and texture of a walnut. Her short, curly hair was dyed a defiant black. Elijah had never seen her without makeup—or without about a pound of jewelry on her wrists and neck. "This isn't my first wildfire—far from it. My husband was a firefighter, you know."

"Yes ma'am," said Elijah. He'd heard a lot about old Mr. Lucas over the past year. A family man, a hard worker—the type of person Marco approved of. Elijah didn't mind listening to Mrs. Lucas's stories about her deceased husband, mostly because Mrs. Lucas was the one telling those stories. He suspected that if old Mr. Lucas had been married to anybody else, he would've seemed kind of boring, even with his death-defying career.

"I'm all packed in case there's an evacuation," Mrs. Lucas went on. "My daughter's driving up from Fern Knoll to get me."

"That's a three-hour drive, Mrs. Lucas."

"She's a fast driver. Just like I used to be." Mrs. Lucas winked.

Elijah laughed. "All right. You just call my uncle if you need anything in the meantime."

"Sure will. I bet your uncle's got enough to worry about, though. I remember when he started building that house. I never saw somebody so proud, so excited."

It was hard to imagine Marco excited. Marco just wasn't that kind of guy. But Elijah did remember when his uncle finally saved enough money to build his own house: Marco had always been tall, but for the first time he seemed to stand up straight.

Elijah remembered when he and his parents had gotten their first tour of the finished house. His uncle knew the place inside out—could've drawn you a map of the electrical wiring or told you the entire history of the bathroom tile. Sure, the house was small. Sure, the furniture was old. But Marco had earned every inch of the place. In a way, it was his life's work.

To lose all that, to start over from scratch . . . Elijah's stomach twisted. "I'm a little worried about him, Mrs. Lucas. He's outside with a hose and a bunch of buckets of water, like he thinks he can scare the fire off or something."

Mrs. Lucas pursed her carefully painted lips. "You make sure he leaves the firefighting to the professionals. It's a lot of trouble for the firefighters when people insist on staying in their homes. Very distracting when they have to rescue people instead of focusing on the fire itself. Tell your uncle to think about that."

"I will, ma'am—thanks."

He looked over his shoulder, south toward Carthage. The smoke already looked closer. Elijah could see a thick column of it, rising above the trees in the distance. He couldn't believe how . . . *detailed* that smoke was. He could see every fold, every ruffle in the white plumes. It was a little like watching milk dissolve in black coffee.

Except that this smoke wasn't contained.

Brenna

"Don't panic," Brenna told Nicole, who was clearly panicking.

"But if there's smoke, there's a fire—"

"Somewhere," Brenna cut her off. "There's a fire *somewhere*. It might not be anywhere near us. You can smell smoke from up to thirty miles away. We might not be in any danger. And even if we are, we still need to stay calm."

Keegan wrinkled his forehead. "Couldn't it just be smoke from a regular campfire? Why should we even assume that there's a wildfire?"

"Because the park has a ban on campfires this time of year," snapped Brenna. "People are only supposed to use gas or propane camp stoves. I explained that before we got here."

"Oh, yeah. Huh." Keegan sniffed again, as if he could smell hidden clues in the smoke. "Well, maybe someone broke the rules."

"That would be a really, really bad idea. Especially at this time of year."

Brenna swung her backpack off her shoulder and pulled out her phone. No service. They'd just have to use their best instincts.

"There's a clearing a little farther up this trail, if I'm remembering right," she said. "We should be able to get a good view from there. If the fire looks close, we can head back to the park entrance where we left my car."

"Are you sure there's actually a clearing up ahead?" asked Keegan.

Here we go again. "Let's find out," she said. "Unless you'd rather turn around and leave right now?"

"No, I'm good. Let's try to get a look."

Nicole bit her lip. "I don't know. Maybe we should just head for the car."

"The clearing's not far, right?" said Keegan. "I mean, the *alleged* clearing."

Mother of . . . Brenna took out her paper map of the park. She unfolded it and pointed to the trail they were on. "We're here, just past that mile-marker. And look, here's an open space about a quarter of a mile away. So, again, if we're walking at three miles an hour—"

"Got it," said Keegan.

"I hope so," Brenna muttered.

They walked on, breathing in smoky air.

***

Five minutes later, they reached the clearing. From the rocky slope where they stood, they could see over miles of treetops.

Directly east of them, narrow tongues of red-orange flame shot up from the trees. Dark gray smoke curled into the sky.

"Whoa," said Nicole.

"That's pretty far away," said Keegan. "And it might not even be heading in our direction."

"True," said Brenna. "In fact, the wind's coming from the south. So it's probably pushing the fire north—not west, toward us."

Keegan nodded, looking satisfied that she agreed with him.

Brenna wasn't finished, though. "But fires can change direction super fast. It all depends on which way the wind's coming from. And even in the last few minutes, I noticed the wind shift at least twice. Which means we can't be too careful. Let's head back to the car."

The smoke thickened in the air as they walked. Nicole coughed.

"Hold on," said Brenna. She pulled out her water bottle and undid the bandanna around her neck. "Guys, pour some water on your bandannas. Once the cloth is damp, we can hold the bandannas against our mouths to help us breathe through the smoke."

Keegan shook his head. "I've heard it's better to use a *dry* cloth. Wet cloth could create steam that burns our lungs."

"Sure, that would be true if we were right in the thick of the fire's heat," said Brenna impatiently. "But for that to be a concern, we'd have to be dealing with temperatures of, like, two hundred degrees Fahrenheit. The fire's not close enough to make the air that hot." *Yet.* "Right now we need to keep the smoke out of our lungs. And a wet cloth will help filter the smoke."

As if to prove Brenna's point, Nicole coughed again.

Keegan frowned at Brenna as if she'd given him a tough riddle to solve—a challenge, instead of the plain facts. "Are you sure about—"

"*Yes I'm sure!*" Brenna exploded. "But if you don't believe me, feel free to keep your cloth dry! Enjoy the smoke inhalation! Which, by the way, is the main cause of death from wildfires. But go ahead, play devil's advocate. You've obviously spent a lot of time learning about this subject—*at least* ten minutes of Internet research, I bet."

If Elijah were here, he wouldn't have to shout at Keegan. He wouldn't have to explain and justify and practically write essays about every little thing. If Elijah were here, they'd probably be back in Brenna's car by now, heading home to safety.

Keegan frowned, took a swig from his water bottle, and silently dribbled a few drops onto his bandanna. Nicole did the same, and they all pulled their moistened bandannas over their mouths.

An orangey-pink tinge seeped into the sky, into the sunlight. Overhead, Brenna saw what looked like floating scraps of blackened paper: ash from the fire, drifting toward them.

Brenna slowed down. *Why are we seeing ash? If the fire's to the west of us, and we're heading south . . . why does it seem like we're getting closer to it?*

A minute later, they saw the other fire. The one that blocked their path to the park entrance.

5

Elijah

"**M**arco, can I have my car key back?" Elijah asked.

Marco was leaning a ladder against the side of the house. "Why? You going somewhere?"

"Not right now," said Elijah. "But if we have to evacuate, shouldn't we both have access to the car?"

Marco narrowed his eyes. "You're still grounded."

"I figured."

Marco reached into his jeans pocket, took out his key ring, and removed the key he'd confiscated from Elijah on

Friday. "Listen, I'm not leaving. If we get an evacuation order, you should take the car and Serafina and get out of here. But I'm staying."

He handed Elijah the car key and turned back to the ladder.

Elijah cleared his throat. "Mrs. Lucas says—"

"I'm not having a conversation about this, Elijah. I've got work to do. Gotta make sure the gutters are totally clean and then fill 'em with water."

What? That's a thing people do?

Maybe it was a thing homeowners did. Elijah didn't know much about that. But he did know a little about what could stop miles of sixty-foot-high flames in their tracks. Fancy helicopters dumping tons of water and flame retardant might do the trick. Or those controlled burns, the backfires that ate up all the possible fuel in a fire's path. Or a massive thunderstorm.

Water-filled gutters and an ordinary guy with a rake? Unlikely.

Elijah looked down at the car key in his hand. He tried to think of a time when he'd managed to change his uncle's mind—about anything.

He drew a blank.

When he glanced at the horizon again, the smoke column looked twice as big.

6

Brenna

The second fire was a lot smaller than the one to the east.

But it was also a lot closer. Five miles away at the most, judging by the landmarks Brenna could still make out. And with the wind this strong, the fire had to be moving at almost ten miles an hour. *One mile every six minutes . . .*

Even from this distance, Brenna could tell that the flames were massive—towers of flickering orange looming above the trees. Lunging forward like soldiers marching in formation, those flames consumed everything in their path. She couldn't see beyond the fire, but she knew what it must be leaving in its wake: a long stretch of blackened, dead earth.

"Where did that come from?" asked Nicole, her voice shrill with fear. "It wasn't there earlier this morning . . . "

"It must've been sparked by floating embers from the main fire," said Brenna. The smoke was thick now, wrapping everything in a grayish mist. Brenna's lungs stung, even with the bandanna over her mouth.

Stay calm. If Elijah were here, he'd stay calm. Elijah loved when nature threw surprises at him. He loved that no matter how much you knew about the wilderness, you could never be sure what it would do next.

Brenna sort of hated that.

At least when it was a matter of life and death.

Elijah would've risen to this challenge. He would've accepted what he couldn't predict and rolled with it.

But Elijah wasn't here.

Brenna was the only non-rookie on this camping trip—even if Keegan wouldn't admit that. It was up to her to get them out of this.

"Okay," she said. "Time for a change of plans."

Nicole gripped Brenna's arm. "What do we do?"

Brenna took a cautious breath. "Well, we obviously can't get to the entrance. So we'll have to take shelter inside the park." She slung her backpack off her shoulder. "We cover up any exposed skin as much as possible. Just in case we run into burning embers from the fire—or anything else that could burn us. Did you guys bring any clothes made of cotton or wool?"

"Wool?" Keegan snorted. "In the middle of summer? Are you serious?"

Brenna sighed. This was actually a fair point. "I'm just asking because a lot of synthetic fabrics can melt really easily and make burns worse. So it's safest to stick to natural fabrics."

"I think my jacket is cotton," said Nicole, digging around in her own backpack.

"Sounds like you're planning for the worst-case scenario," said Keegan.

Brenna raised her eyebrows at him. "When the worst-case scenario seems pretty likely to happen, it's a good idea to plan for it. Don't you agree?"

"But where do we *go?*" pressed Nicole.

Brenna took a light cotton sweater out of her backpack and pulled it over her head before answering the question. "The safest place would be a big body of water."

"So, Topaz Lake?" said Nicole shakily, pulling out her jacket and checking the tag. "Or the creek on the way to Nero Canyon?"

"We should head back north to the creek," said Keegan. "That's closer to us than the lake."

"But the route to the creek is uphill," said Brenna. "Fire travels way faster uphill. The lake is downhill—"

"But the creek is farther away from the fire."

"The lake's west of us. This fire's to the south. And the wind's blowing mostly from south to north—toward us. So if we head west toward the lake, we'll be moving perpendicular to the fire. Which is actually the safest direction to move in this kind of situation. Nobody can outrun a wildfire for very long, so moving in the exact opposite direction doesn't do a lot of good."

"But the creek is closer to us," Keegan protested again.

"Not by much. It's a mile and a half away. The lake's only two miles away. We can be there in less than half an hour if we move fast. And it's the safer option. A fire this big could easily jump the creek and surround us. The lake's a much bigger barrier."

"I still don't think—" Keegan started.

Nicole cut him off. "You know what, Keegan? Shut up." She zipped up the jacket she'd just put on and shouldered her backpack. "Brenna knows what she's talking about."

Huh, thought Brenna. *Didn't see that coming.*

They veered off the trail and jogged through the trees, moving along uneven ground scattered with brownish vegetation. Brenna watched her compass, making sure they stayed on track. Keegan held his compass too. He kept glancing between it and Brenna. Brenna felt as if they were in a bad TV show, where Keegan was some kind of super-spy and Brenna was a suspected double agent. Like she wasn't tense enough already.

Why did he have to make such a show of not trusting her judgment?

Why were they friends? She wished she could remember.

She wished Elijah were here.

Elijah's not here. You're here—and you can do this.

They jogged along the edge of a narrow ravine. Overhead, above the sparse canopy of tree branches, birds carpeted the pinkish sky. *They're all flying in the same direction we're going,* Brenna noticed. *West—perpendicular to the second fire. So I must've made the right call.*

Nicole surged forward, breaking into a full run. Not smart, thought Brenna. *We should be saving our energy.* Sprinting away from a fire was like using a fork to fend off attackers. It might work, but only as a last resort. And not if you had to keep it up for hours.

"Careful," Brenna warned Nicole. "Watch where you're going."

"Come on, Brenna," said Keegan, who was also speeding up. "Quit telling everyone what to do. Do you have to act like you know everythi—"

His voice broke off as his foot slipped.

Brenna froze—and watched in horror as Keegan plunged sideways into the ravine.

Elijah

"This is a very fast-moving, wind-driven fire," announced the news anchor. "In just a few hours it's grown from a hundred acres to more than six thousand acres. Wind gusts are pushing it farther north at a speed of more than ten miles an hour."

"This doesn't look good," Elijah remarked to Serafina. The dog ignored him, as usual.

The reporter continued, "At this time, the fire is only five percent contained. More than thirty homes in Carthage have been destroyed. A temporary evacuation center is being set up at the county fairgrounds . . . "

Elijah looked around the living room. The obvious things were already in his duffel: a few changes of clothes, toothbrush and toothpaste, deodorant, razor. But what if the house and everything in it actually burned? This wasn't like packing for an overnight trip. This was like packing for an entire life.

His pulse spiked. "Crap," he said to Serafina. Serafina rolled onto her side.

Elijah pulled out his phone and looked up directions to the county fairgrounds. It should be pretty easy to get there, if they just drove straight through downtown Hayden and then kept going east. They could be there in twenty minutes if they took either Park Drive or Rochester Avenue. Elijah saved both routes in his phone.

Then he got to work.

He moved quickly from room to room. Stuffed more clothes into his duffel and his school backpack. Filled a trash bag with any food that wouldn't spoil. Tossed in Serafina's food and water bowls, a bag of her dog food, her heartworm medicine, and the snacks that were good for her teeth. Carried everything to the car and loaded up the trunk. There was still room for a couple more bags in there, plus they had the whole backseat.

"What else?" he asked Serafina when he got back into the house. The dog let out a bored groan.

"Well, maybe you're not sentimental, but I am."

He started gathering things. The pictures on the walls, his basketball trophy, that stupid certificate from his sixth-grade science fair. His dad's letters from prison, holiday cards from his mom. Everything went into his camping backpack, along with his water bottle, shampoo, and a towel. Band-Aids, a pack of tissues. His smaller game consoles.

He should probably pack Marco's stuff too, since Marco seemed to have other priorities right now.

When Elijah went into his uncle's room, Serafina noticed. She came and sat by the door, watching him suspiciously.

"I'm just getting some of his clothes, okay?" Elijah said to her. "And, like, his contact case and toothbrush. Quit looking at me like I'm robbing the place."

The dog didn't seem convinced. She followed him around as he put his uncle's stuff into a fresh trash bag.

Elijah snapped his fingers. "Cell phone chargers! Almost forgot those."

Serafina raised and lowered her floppy ears, unimpressed.

He kept thinking of new things to bring. It made him nervous—made him wonder what he was still forgetting. He took out his phone and did an Internet search for *fire evacuation things to take.*

"Don't judge me," he told Serafina. "If you had opposable thumbs, you'd do the same thing."

***

As Elijah stepped outside, he heard sirens. Somewhere nearby, fire trucks were screeching their way south.

Elijah's uncle was done messing with the gutters. Now he was just standing in the front yard, holding the hose the way some people held guns. Everything about Marco's posture said *Come and get me.*

Elijah didn't want to think what might happen if the fire took Marco up on that dare.

"Hey, Marco, where's the deed for the house?"

"What?"

"You know, the deed. The paper that says you own the house, or whatever? Where do you keep it?"

"Why do you care?"

"Just in case we have to leave and . . . you know, the house . . . gets damaged. It would be good to have that paperwork."

Elijah heard a helicopter overhead. He looked up in time to see the chopper fly by, heading south toward the fire. *Those backfires probably didn't work*, Elijah thought. *Must be time for the water-spraying helicopters.*

Could backfires backfire? Stupid thing to be wondering about right now. He focused on his uncle again.

Marco sighed. "Elijah, this isn't your problem. I told you, I'll do whatever I have to do to protect this house. I'll defend it with my life."

"Yeah," muttered Elijah. "That's what I'm afraid of."

Brenna

"**K**eegan!" Brenna shouted. She and Nicole made their way down the slope as fast as they could without falling themselves. The walls of the ravine were steep, but trees and thick underbrush gave them handholds.

Keegan lay at the bottom of the ravine, curled into a tight ball. His backpack lay a couple feet away. Thick smoke pooled around them, trapped between the ravine walls.

"Keegan! Are you okay?" shrieked Nicole.

Keegan made an angry noise that sort of answered the question.

Brenna and Nicole knelt down on either side of him. His right arm was bent at a painful-looking angle. He clutched at it with his other hand. No sign of his compass. He must've dropped it as he fell.

"Talk to us, Keegan," she said. "Can you sit up?"

He did, slowly, cradling his injured arm against his chest like a broken wing. "I can't move my arm."

Brenna sucked in her breath. "Well, that's . . . not great."

"Gahhhh, yeah. Yeah, that hurts." He gritted his teeth and shut his eyes.

"Okay, don't worry. You're going to be fine. Just hold still." She took a closer look at his arm. It was badly bruised and starting to swell. There was a lump below his elbow. Definitely a broken bone.

Brenna pulled out her phone. If they could just manage to call 9-1-1 . . .

She still didn't have cell service. "Nicole, are you getting any bars?"

Nicole checked her phone. "No, nothing."

She sounded as if she might cry—not that Brenna would blame her at this point. "What do we do now?"

Brenna looked at Keegan. He was hunched over, shaking with pain. She doubted he'd be able to get very far like this.

"Keegan, I think your arm's broken," she said gently. "I think we can reset the bone and make a splint for you. That way you'll be in less pain, okay?"

Are you sure? No. She wasn't sure about anything. That was the problem.

She'd never set a broken bone before. She'd only learned how to do it in the first aid class she took ages ago.

And she'd never performed any kind of first aid with a wildfire breathing down her neck.

The air around them was neon orange now. Brenna heard a rumbling in the distance. The sound of flames and wind racing closer. Her bandanna had dried out, and she couldn't tell if it was blocking much of the smoke. Either way, the smoke was definitely getting thicker, and it was getting harder to breathe.

If Elijah were here . . .

He wouldn't be sure either. There was no way to be sure. She just had to do her best. That was all anyone could do in a situation like this.

Brenna swallowed the ash in her throat. "Nicole, I need you to find me two really straight, sturdy sticks—about this long." She used two fingers to mark off the space between Keegan's wrist and elbow.

Nicole launched into her search as Brenna dug around in Keegan's overstuffed backpack. "Stay really still, Keegan. You're doing great." She pulled out one of his pocket knives and the roll of nylon rope. That material wouldn't hold up well if the fire caught up to them, but she didn't have anything else to work with. A moment later, Nicole was back with two sticks.

"These are perfect," said Brenna. "Awesome work. Now for the fun part."

Resetting the bone to its proper position quickly earned a spot on Brenna's list of

Things She Never Wanted to Do Again. The look on Keegan's face—the *feeling* of the bone popping back into place—made her want to throw up. But then it was done, and the agony in Keegan's eyes immediately started to fade. It only took another minute to make the splint. Brenna cut pieces of rope and tied the sticks in place, on either side of Keegan's arm.

"That feels *so* much better," Keegan gasped. Then he coughed. With his good hand, he adjusted his bandanna.

No time to celebrate. Brenna shoved the knife and rope back in Keegan's bag.

"We have to get out of this ravine," she said. "If the fire catches up to us here, it'll feed off the wind tunnel in here and trap us."

For once, Keegan didn't look doubtful. He didn't challenge her. He just stood up, picked up his backpack with his good arm, and nodded. "Well, my legs are working fine. Let's go." He paused, then added, "Lead the way, Brenna."

9

Elijah

"We now have reports that secondary fires have started in Topaz State Park," said the TV anchor. "The park is being evacuated, but it's possible that some hikers are trapped in remote areas. Rescue helicopters are sweeping the area . . . "

Elijah stared at the TV. Brenna. Keegan and Nicole. What if they're stranded? Or hurt? Or . . . He sent another text to his friends and then called Brenna's mom.

That was a mistake. She was panicked. "I haven't heard anything from her either! I wanted to drive up to the park and try to find her, but—"

"That's a terrible idea," said Elijah.

Brenna's mother took a sobby breath. "I know, I know. I'm just so afraid something's happened to them. And now we might have to evacuate . . . "

"It's going to be okay," Elijah told her. "Cell phone service out at Topaz is always a joke. I'm sure Brenna and the others are fine. Brenna knows that place like the back of her hand. She won't do anything stupid or dangerous. Can you let me know when you hear from her, though?"

Brenna's mom promised she would. Elijah hung up and tried to think about something other than his friends' safety. Something he could control.

Weird—Brenna was the one who liked having things under control. Elijah usually preferred to just go with the flow. To let things happen. To not sweat the small stuff or the big stuff. Because the big stuff was usually too big to handle.

But he had to do something right now.

His phone battery was starting to run low,

so he fished his charger out of his backpack and plugged it in. Then he looked at Serafina. "If I were an important document, where would I be?"

The dog's ears tented upward—the canine version of a shrug.

"Thanks. Super helpful."

It felt wrong to search his uncle's room. Whenever Marco searched Elijah's room, Elijah wanted to punch a wall. Not that there was anything for Marco to find, but everyone deserved some private space.

So much for that. Elijah opened Marco's dresser drawers, checked the shelf in his closet, even looked under the bed. He felt like an idiot. But Marco had worked so hard, sacrificed so much, to build this house. If it went up in flames, Marco would need proof that he owned the property. He'd have to file insurance claims and jump through hoops Elijah could barely imagine. The least Elijah could do was save the crucial paperwork.

He could hear the TV in the living room. "The sheriff's department is now issuing a mandatory evacuation notice for the towns of

Diamond Ridge and Hayden . . . "

This is it.

"We don't have much time," Elijah said to Serafina.

Serafina turned around and trotted back to the living room.

He'd just have to ask Marco again. He'd tell his uncle about the mandatory evacuation. He'd find a way to make him understand . . .

As Elijah crossed the living room on the way to the front door, Serafina let out a low growl.

This dog wasn't a growler. Growling was beneath her. Elijah paused. She was sitting in front of the game cabinet again. All his and Marco's gaming systems were in there. Marco had these huge, ancient consoles from the eighties and nineties . . .

Elijah knelt down in front of the cabinet. He moved aside a few of the outdated monster-sized consoles on the top shelf. Nothing there. He tried the lower shelf. No luck.

Wait . . .

Elijah put his hand on the underside of the top shelf and felt something soft. A moment later he pulled out the manila envelope that had been taped there.

Inside the envelope was a stack of official-looking papers. Elijah flipped through them at light-speed. There were his custody papers—his birth certificate— medical records. And, yes, the deed to Marco's property.

Mission accomplished. Elijah leapt to his feet. "Good work, girl! Seriously, we could have our own TV show or something."

Serafina leveled her beady brown dog eyes at him, like, *Please*.

Elijah raced outside.

"Marco! We gotta go! The mandatory evacuation got issued! Come on!"

The sky had changed color. The orange had deepened, turning from a sunset shade to a sort of glowing darkness, like hot charcoal. Elijah suddenly felt that he wasn't standing out in the open at all. He was trapped under a dome of rust-colored smoke.

A dull roaring noise filled the air. And Elijah saw the flames, no more than half a mile away, flowing into Hayden as fast as a rushing river.

"It's here! Marco, it's right here!"

Brenna

Scrambling out of the ravine took a while. Keegan's injured arm made the climb harder for him, so Brenna and Nicole took turns supporting him. When they reached the top, Nicole said, "We should all be drinking water. Isn't it super important to stay hydrated in situations like this?"

"You're right," said Brenna. So Nicole wasn't totally clueless about surviving in the wilderness after all. Brenna tried not to let her surprise show. Maybe she'd been underestimating the others the same way Keegan had underestimated her.

They sipped from their water bottles as they jogged west. A few minutes later, Brenna felt the change in the wind. *No. No no no . . .*

"Guys, not to make this day even worse, but . . . I think the wind is shifting again."

"Yeah," agreed Keegan. "It's coming out of the east now, isn't it?"

"Yeah." Meaning it was blowing the fire west—the same way they were moving.

"That could be a good thing, though, right?" said Nicole. "If the fire's to the south, and it just starts moving west, it'll be parallel to us. It won't catch up to us that way."

"True," said Brenna. "The problem is the other fire."

The bigger fire. The one to the east of them.

Nicole gasped, so Brenna figured she understood.

The bigger fire was moving directly toward them now.

More shreds of ash drifted out of the sky. Thousands of embers, glowing like fireflies, skittered along the ground, blowing ahead of the fire. They landed on bushes, tree branches, grass. Mini-fires had ignited on all sides. Brenna felt the heat building. She was sweating through her light sweater. The stray hairs at the nape of her neck—strands too short for her ponytail—were plastered to her damp skin. Brenna's phone burned in her jeans pocket. She pulled it out, wondering if it was getting fried. Some cell phones overheated and exploded if you covered them with a pillow. Brenna slipped her phone into the mesh side pocket of her backpack. At least if it exploded there, it wouldn't take her thigh with it.

The sky's orange hue deepened, and the approaching flames combined with the wind to create a deep roar—a sound that reminded Brenna of the revving of a jet engine. A sound that kept getting louder.

"Look out!" shouted Nicole. She grabbed Brenna's arm and yanked her sideways. An instant later, a flaming tree branch landed inches from Brenna.

"Thanks," Brenna gasped. She doubted Nicole even heard her above the noise.

They kept going. A minute later, Brenna glanced down at her compass to make sure they were still on course.

That was her mistake.

If she'd seen the falling tree half a second sooner, she would've dodged it completely.

As it toppled, she tried to veer out of the way. But the trunk clipped her backpack, throwing off her weight. She felt herself falling, twisting in midair as she lost her balance.

She felt herself land.

She didn't feel the tree land on her lower right leg. Not right away, at least.

She just tried to keep moving and realized she couldn't. She lay on the ground in an awkward sprawl, like a failed snow angel. Her foot was pinned under the tree trunk.

Which was on fire.

Nicole and Keegan were both shouting—screaming, technically. Brenna heard Keegan yell, "We have to put the flames out first! Use your jacket!"

Nicole dropped her backpack and peeled off her jacket. She and Keegan both beat at the tree trunk with the fabric. Gradually they smothered the flames near Brenna's leg. Then they knelt down next to the trunk.

"We're going to get this off you, Brenna," Keegan said. "Just give us a second."

"Be careful." Brenna didn't recognize her own voice. It sounded like the voice of someone who'd been smoking for fifty years. Or someone who was being strangled. "It's got to weigh close to a hundred pounds." How did she know that, when she couldn't even feel it sitting on top of her? Certain parts of her brain must be running loose, doing work without her.

Keegan looked at Nicole. "I don't think I can get a good grip, with my arm . . . "

"It's okay," said Nicole grimly. "I've got this. Brenna, do you think you can move your leg, once the tree's out of the way?"

"Um . . . I'm not sure it'll move on its own. But I can pull myself clear with my arms, as long as you get the weight off it."

"I'll help you," said Keegan. Crouching beside her, he wrapped his good arm around her waist. "Whenever you say, Nicole."

"Okay then—here we go." Nicole wrapped her arms around the scorched trunk and heaved up. "Now!"

Brenna felt the trunk lift off her leg. She felt Keegan pulling her backward before she could even think about moving. And then, finally, she felt the pain. It rushed into her lower leg all at once. She wanted to scream, but she could barely get enough breath for a decent gasp.

When Brenna was clear, Nicole let the trunk drop back to the ground with a thud.

"You're *not* gonna be able to stand on that," Keegan said firmly. For once, Brenna completely agreed with him.

"We have to move, though," she choked out. "Help me up. Leave my backpack behind."

She wriggled out of her backpack straps, trying not to think about the gear she'd lose. Nicole grabbed Brenna's water bottle and phone, forcing Brenna to sip some water before shoving both items in her own backpack. Then Keegan and Nicole got on either side of her and gently eased her upright. The three of them staggered in place. Brenna tried to balance on her good leg but found herself leaning heavily on Nicole. Keegan coughed on a lungful of ash.

This might be easier if we could all at least breathe, Brenna thought.

"Guess it's your turn to break a bone now, Nicole," said Keegan.

"Not even funny," said Nicole. She held up Brenna's compass, which she must've picked up off the ground. "West is that way. Come on."

***

Five minutes later, they were all wheezing from the smoke. Brenna's brain seemed to have split in two. One half was calculating wind direction, wind speed, distances. The other half was howling in pain, almost loudly enough to drown out the sound of the fire as it barreled toward them.

We're moving too slowly. I'm moving too slowly.

They reached another clearing—a wide patch of bare, rocky ground. No trees within a hundred-foot radius. Hardly any shrubs or even grass. Not much that would feed the fire when it passed through.

This spot might be her best chance.

"Guys," she said, "listen. I'm not going to make it to the lake."

Elijah

Marco still hadn't moved.

"Mrs. Lucas hasn't left yet!" he called to Elijah. "Ask her if she needs a ride."

Elijah ran next door.

He pounded on Mrs. Lucas's front door until she answered. "Mrs. Lucas, you heard that we got the evacuation order?"

"Yes. My daughter's on her way, but—"

"How far away is she?"

"It'll be another half hour before she gets here."

Elijah drew in his breath. "That settles it, then. You're coming with us."

***

Elijah heaved Mrs. Lucas's two suitcases into the trunk of Marco's car. He might have to sit on the trunk lid to close it . . .

The smoke had followed him into the garage. He coughed. Mrs. Lucas was already wearing a paper face mask. She held a lightweight blanket in her arms. "This is one hundred percent cotton," she told him. "Cotton and wool are the most fire-resistant fabrics. If worse comes to worst, we throw this over our heads and cross our fingers."

Elijah thought about throwing the blanket over Marco's head. Maybe that would confuse his uncle long enough for Elijah to drag him to the car.

"You really are prepared for this," he said to Mrs. Lucas. "Way better prepared than we are."

"Young man, I've lived in the Southwest all my life. Even before I met my husband, I'd seen my share of fires."

Elijah grinned. As terrified as he was, Mrs. Lucas seemed impossibly calm. He hoped some of that calmness would rub off on him.

"And I bet those fires were smart enough not to mess with you."

She winked at him. "Most of them."

***

Serafina didn't want to leave. The moment Elijah clipped her leash to her collar, she sat down firmly. Her expression reminded him of Marco's.

"Come on, girl," said Elijah. He tugged on the leash with one hand, clutching his phone and charger in the other hand. If they were lucky, it would be a matter of minutes before the fire reached their house.

And if they weren't lucky . . .

"Seriously, Serafina," he said, getting desperate. He didn't dare try to pick the dog up. He'd tried that once, months ago. She'd head-butted him hard enough to give him a concussion. "We're running out of time. And I still have to convince Marco to leave. Work with me here."

The dog's ears rose at the sound of her owner's name.

"Yeah. Marco. He's outside. We need to get him. Trust me, girl, you don't want any of us to be here when that fire shows up."

Serafina stood up and followed him.

***

Elijah pulled the car out of the garage, into the driveway. With Mrs. Lucas and Serafina in the backseat, he just had one more passenger to pick up. "Marco! You can't beat that thing back! The firefighters will do everything they can to save the house. We gotta go! Now!"

"You go ahead with Mrs. Lucas. I'll be fine—"

"Marco, it's not worth it!"

"Don't you dare tell me what's not worth it!" Marco yelled.

Something snapped, deep inside Elijah's chest. In his mind, he saw firefighters setting their own fires, backfires that were supposed to stop the main blaze in its tracks—fires that succeeded only in creating more destruction. Lines of defense that failed, leaving people in more danger than ever. "Do you want to die? Because that's what will happen if you stay here. I bet you'll feel like a real hero then, when you burn to a crisp. That's not brave, Marco. That's just stupid. And leaving isn't cowardly. It's just what we have to do."

Marco glared at him with a look of pure rage. "You didn't work for this! You didn't sacrifice for this! I don't abandon the things I care about! I'm not a quitter like—"

He didn't finish, but he didn't have to.

I'm not a quitter like your parents. Like you.

Elijah took a deep breath. Smoke snaked down his throat and into his lungs, burning the whole way. "Marco, I know this house has always been your dream. Of course you don't want to lose that. But what matters more—this house, or our lives? We need you, Marco. You're not going to abandon *us*, are you? You're not going to leave us in the lurch, right? Because I don't know what we'll do then. I really don't. Please. We're counting on you, man."

Marco stared at Elijah like he didn't recognize him. Then he looked back at the house. Then back at Elijah.

Serafina let out a whimper. Elijah had hardly ever heard her make a noise. First that growl when he was looking for the documents, and now this.

Marco's eyes swiveled back to the car. Without a word, he set down the hose and climbed into the passenger's seat.

Elijah didn't gun the engine, in case it stalled. Instead he eased the car forward and gradually added speed. He had a feeling Serafina's whimper had done more to change Marco's mind than his own speech. He'd have to remember to give Serafina one of those dental treats she liked.

If they made it out of this alive.

12

Brenna

Brenna dropped to the ground and crawled to the center of the clearing. It was a little easier to breathe closer to the ground. That helped her think. In her head, she marked off the size of the hole she would need.

Three feet wide, a little more than five feet long.

About the size of a coffin.

"Keegan, I need your shovel."

"What?"

"Your shovel!" she shouted over the thunder of the oncoming fire. "From your backpack! Give it to me!"

Keegan just gaped at her. Nicole stepped behind Keegan, unzipped his backpack, and found the shovel. She handed it to Brenna, her eyes confused. "Why do you need this?"

"Don't worry. Just head for the lake."

Nicole finally registered what Brenna meant to do. Her face flashed with the same disbelief and horror that already filled Keegan's eyes. "What? We're not leaving you behind! We'll carry you!"

Brenna started digging. The dirt was hard-packed and dry from the months without rain, but Keegan's shovel cut through it easily. "Dragging me will slow you down. We'll *all* get caught by the fire. You need to run. Now."

"No way!"

"Look, I might be okay here. This space right here is pretty open. There's not much vegetation. The fire won't have much to eat when it gets here."

"Except *you*!" shrieked Nicole. Brenna didn't look up, but she could tell from Nicole's voice that her friend was starting to cry.

"I'm going to dig a hole and cover myself with dirt," Brenna explained. "People have survived that way."

"That's a long shot," said Keegan. "Come on, if you just let us help you walk—"

"There's no time!" Brenna shouted. She dug with fierce speed, tossing mini-mounds of soil off to the side. Spikes of pain shot through her leg, but she couldn't afford to slow down.

Nicole knelt and started clawing at the ground with her hands. Frantically, she tore up clumps of parched dirt and flung them off to the side.

"This is insane!" yelled Keegan. Not like before, when he'd disagreed just for the sake of it. Now he *meant* it. Still, he too got down on his knees and started scooping out fistfuls of dirt. "You can't dig a hole deep enough—"

"Simple math." Brenna huffed out the words between stabs of the shovel. "The lake is a mile away. You're both average runners, so if you run, you can get there in less than ten minutes. With me, it'll take you closer to twenty minutes. The fire's got to be traveling at about ten miles an hour, and it's half a mile away at the most. So it'll be at this spot in about three minutes. It'll get to the lake in less than ten minutes. In other words, there's enough time for you two to get to the lake, but not me. But if I dig nine inches deeper each minute for three minutes, I'll have a hole that's more than two feet deep. Which is deep enough for me to fit into."

"You didn't factor in the extra time you'll need to cover yourself with dirt," Keegan pointed out. Even now, he couldn't seem to help himself. "And nine inches per minute doesn't seem realis—"

"Shut up and RUN FOR THE LAKE!"

"Brenna—" Nicole started.

Brenna gave her a shove. "*GOOOOOOO!*"

With his good arm, Keegan pulled Nicole to her feet, and they both ran.

Brenna was relieved.

Because she was pretty sure she was going to die in two and half minutes. And if they started running now, they probably wouldn't hear her scream.

Elijah

Elijah was driving through fire.

Pockets of flame licked the rain-starved grass on either side of Park Drive. But those little clusters weren't the whole fire. They were just sideshows started by drifting embers. The main attraction was behind them, sounding like Godzilla piped through loudspeakers. And by the sound of it, Elijah could tell it was gaining on them fast.

Ahead of them, shapes materialized through the smoke: sawhorses straddling the road. "Great," growled Elijah. "A roadblock. Guess we're going with the backup route."

He turned right on Drexel and then headed up Rochester, through the center of town. But the situation didn't improve much. Even with the headlights on, he was losing visibility. A dull reddish haze of smoke swallowed the street.

With a jolt, the car's front right tire slammed into something.

"Gahh!" Elijah stepped on the brakes.

"You hit the curb," said Marco tensely.

"Sorry." He'd had no idea he'd veered that far from the center of his lane.

Elijah rolled back off the curb and moved to the left. At this point he was driving so slowly that a kid on a scooter could've outpaced him. Not to mention the wildfire. Any second now, the main front would be right on top of them.

I need to get off the road, Elijah realized. *Ideally, in a spot where we won't be prime fire bait.*

Through the smoke he spotted the outline of a familiar brick building up ahead. The post office. The building itself would be closed and locked up because of the evacuation, so there was no chance of taking shelter inside. But the parking lot was a little oasis of asphalt—no trees or grass to feed the approaching flames. And almost anywhere was safer than the middle of the road.

Elijah guessed at the location of the parking lot entrance and pulled over off the road. He must've estimated well, because he didn't hit the sidewalk curb. Or anything else. He pulled up close to the building, figuring the brick wall might help block some of the heat. Then he hit the brakes.

"What are you doing?" shouted Marco.

"I can't keep going! I can't see anything! Who knows what we might hit if I try to drive blind? Anything could be on the road ahead of us—a downed power line, a fallen tree, parked cars . . . It's way too dangerous."

"But what other option do we have?" demanded Marco.

Elijah glanced back at Mrs. Lucas. "The cross-your-fingers option."

He engaged the parking brake.

"What are you doing?" Marco demanded.

"We can't outrun this thing on foot!"

"Definitely not," Elijah agreed. "We're dead if we step out of this car. We need to stay in here."

"I agree," said Mrs. Lucas, sounding as unfazed as ever.

Elijah shot her a grateful look. "Let's get on the floor. We'll be able to breathe better closer to the ground. Come on! Hurry!"

"Leave the engine running," said Mrs. Lucas. "That's what my husband always said to do if I ever found myself in this situation."

"What if the gas tank explodes from the heat?" said Marco.

"That doesn't usually happen," Mrs. Lucas assured him, as if she did this all the time.

Elijah crawled out of the driver's seat and into the back. "Mrs. Lucas, do you think you can lie down on the floor? I'll help you."

"No problem," said Mrs. Lucas, unbuckling her seatbelt.

Elijah grabbed the blanket Mrs. Lucas held in her lap. He tossed it to his uncle. "Marco, get back here!"

Elijah steadied Mrs. Lucas as she lowered herself to the floor. Then he crouched down beside her. "Lie on top of me, Marco. And put the blanket over all of us."

Marco scrambled to join them in the space between the seats. Serafina, who was still sitting in the backseat, let out a whimper. "Hey, girl," Elijah murmured. He reached up, over Mrs. Lucas, and stroked the dog's fur. "Lie down on the seat for me. Down, girl." Serafina stretched herself out across the length of the backseat. Her head rested between her paws, a few inches above Mrs. Lucas's frizzy hair. "Good girl," Elijah said. He kept his hand on the dog's back.

A moment later, the blanket blocked his sight.

Elijah felt the weight of his uncle's body on top of him. He might suffocate just from that. Marco was a heavy guy.

Elijah's hand was still resting on Serafina's warm body. The dog started to shake. "It's okay, girl," Elijah said. "We're here. We're all here."

And one way or another, they weren't going anywhere.

14

Brenna

The earth shook beneath Brenna. The wind
was so hot and so strong that she pictured it
peeling the skin off her face. And all she heard
was the roar of the flames.

She stopped digging and threw her shovel
aside. As carefully as she could, she rolled
into the trench she had dug. It was more of a
shallow dent in the ground, like a flowerbed.
She reached up to sweep her arm over the
displaced dirt outside the hole. It showered
over her in clumps. It didn't feel like much—
especially considering that it was the only
thing standing between her and a wildfire.

The heat was practically crisping the hair off her outstretched arm. She tucked both arms around her head and tried to make her body as small as possible. Through her bandanna, she tried to breathe somewhat normally. Her leg throbbed with a dull pain that would've been unbearable under normal circumstances.

All around her, she could hear the fire, surging forward with the wind, eating everything in its path.

And then it felt as if a giant vacuum had sucked all the oxygen out of the air. So much for trying to breathe.

I hope Nicole and Keegan make it to the lake, she thought.

I hope my family is okay. I hope they forgive me for getting myself killed out here.

I hope this doesn't hurt too much.

Elijah

Smoke seeped through the car's closed windows. Even with the blanket over him, Elijah fought for breath. He could feel Mrs. Lucas breathing shallowly next to him—more shallowly with each minute. In his head, he apologized to Mrs. Lucas's daughter for not leaving sooner.

It was so hot. Unbearably hot. Elijah felt as if his sweat was evaporating the moment it formed. He worked his phone out of his pocket and dialed 9-1-1.

"Hey, yeah, I'm trapped in a vehicle somewhere near the corner of Drexel and

Rochester. The northeast side of Hayden, yeah. We're surrounded by the wildfire . . . And I've got an elderly lady with me . . . yes, ma'am, we're staying right here . . . "

Serafina whimpered again—a high-pitched whine that cut through the low drumroll of the flames and the wind. Elijah mentally apologized to her too. His hand was still buried in her fur—not petting her anymore, just holding on. The same way Marco was gripping Elijah's shoulder.

The car rocked back and forth, pummeled by the wind.

So hot.

"We're gonna roast to death in here!" yelled Marco. Elijah had never heard so much terror in his uncle's voice. "I'm getting out!"

Elijah felt Marco's weight shifting, moving off him. The blanket slipped to one side. Elijah raised his head just in time to see his uncle lunge toward the side door.

"Marco, no!" Elijah dropped his phone and grabbed his uncle's arm as Marco reached for the door handle. "You can't get out now! You'll die out there for sure!"

Marco could easily pull away from him if he wanted to. The guy regularly bench-pressed twice Elijah's weight. "Listen, Marco, the 9-1-1 lady says we'll be okay if we just stay calm. The important thing is not to panic. Here—talk to her. Get the phone for me. It's on the floor in front of you."

Marco was breathing hard, and his eyes had a wild look. But slowly, almost unwillingly, his gaze drifted down to phone on the floor.

"Yeah, right there. Pick it up, Marco. Talk to the dispatcher."

Marco picked up the phone and put it to his ear. Elijah gently pulled him back down onto the floor and threw the blanket back over their heads.

The heat grew more intense with each second, like a giant invisible fist that squeezed him more and more tightly. Without the 9-1-1 dispatcher speaking into his ear, Elijah had to imagine what she would say.

Do not pass out. Do not pass out. Breathe in. Breathe out. You can do this.

Just like Marco said. We do what we have to do.

Brenna

Brenna's mouth tasted of ash. Her lungs burned. She was shaking all over.

But she was alive.

Simple math and a lot of luck.

She'd lost track of how long she'd been lying on the ground, trying to breathe through the searing heat. It could've been five minutes or half an hour. Now, finally, the horrible pressure of the scorching air had faded. Brenna waited until the temperature dropped to a bearable level. Then she sat up and pulled herself out of the hole, ignoring the pain that shot through her leg. The air was easier to breathe once she raised herself a couple of feet off the ground. Weird, considering that the opposite would've been true a few seconds ago.

The smoke was still thick enough to knit a sweater with. Wind whipped against her face and rushed on, chasing the fire. But at least it was quiet now. And she didn't see any flames near her. This rocky patch of ground didn't look much different than it had before, actually.

But beyond it, in every direction she looked, she saw charred trees.

Then she looked up.

And saw the helicopter.

With the last of her strength, Brenna waved frantically at the sky. If her luck hadn't completely run out yet, the pilot would spot the bright red fabric of her sweater.

***

It turned out to be a rescue chopper, and there was just enough room for it to land in the clearing. Within minutes, Brenna was aboard, with her leg in a splint. "My friends," she told the medical team. "They're at Lake Topaz. Or at least I hope they are."

The helicopter headed west. Before today, Brenna would've thought the noise of the rotors was deafening. But now she knew what deafening noise actually sounded like—and smelled like and tasted like.

Echoes of the fire still clung to her lungs. The medics had told her that she needed treatment for smoke inhalation, along with the broken leg and the burns on her back. She was just starting to feel the sting of those burns, which the medics said were surprisingly minor.

As they flew closer to the lake, Brenna closed her eyes. *Please be there. Please be alive.*

"I see two figures in the lake," announced the pilot.

Brenna opened her eyes and laughed. The laugh turned into a cough, but she didn't mind.

Elijah

The heat just *ended*—as if someone had flipped a switch. Elijah could suddenly breathe again. His lungs were still barbecued, but cooler air was entering them.

He raised his head. Sweat trickled down his forehead, into his eyes. He blinked away the sting.

"Marco?" he croaked.

"Polo," said his uncle.

Elijah groaned. "Seriously, man. You're embarrassing yourself. And sit up before you crush my spine." Marco rolled off him, and Elijah raised himself a few inches. "Mrs. Lucas? You okay?"

"So far, so good," she said. Her voice was raspy but as calm as ever.

Elijah looked over at Serafina. The dog raised her head, panting. "How about you, girl?" He stroked one of her ears, and she licked his hand. "Well, that's a first," he said with a shaky laugh. "So that's all it takes for us to bond? If I'd known, I would've driven us into a wildfire sooner."

They stumbled out of the car, which wasn't nearly as badly damaged as Elijah had expected. A few seconds ago, he'd been sure that the frame was melting like cake icing. Now, he could see that the tires and the windows were in bad shape, but the body of the vehicle was intact. Still, it clearly wasn't drivable.

Everything around them was burned. All the buildings along Rochester Avenue looked trashed. Even the brick foundation of the post office had scorch marks. Elijah wondered how much would be left of Hayden when the fire was finished with it.

He didn't let himself think about Marco's house.

Marco climbed into the back, dropped the seat, and started retrieving stuff from the trunk. Touching the outside of the trunk didn't seem wise.

Elijah was still on the phone with the 9-1-1 dispatcher. "Yes, ma'am, we'll wait right here for an ambulance . . . We're all a little wheezy, but otherwise I think we're okay. Yeah, I agree we should all get checked out for smoke inhalation . . . "

He had Serafina's leash wrapped around the hand that held the phone. With his other hand he gripped Mrs. Lucas's arm.

"I'm not about to keel over, you know," she said.

"Oh, I know," he assured her. "It's not you I'm worried about. It's me. I might pass out at any second."

While they waited for the ambulance, Marco called Mrs. Lucas's daughter to let her know what had happened. When he handed the phone to Mrs. Lucas so she could talk to her daughter, Elijah thought, *My mom. I should call my mom . . .*

He would talk to her later, once the ambulance showed up and he could end the call with the 9-1-1 dispatcher. For now, the family he needed most was right here.

"Bless you," Mrs. Lucas said to Marco as she returned his phone. Then she looked at Elijah. "And you, young man. I think you saved all our lives."

"We'll call it a team effort," said Elijah. Serafina breathed a puff of air into his hand. He figured that meant she approved.

***

Ten minutes later, all of them were in an ambulance on their way to the hospital. Mrs. Lucas had bullied the paramedics into letting Serafina ride along. Marco brought Mrs. Lucas's bags, and Elijah took his backpack and duffel. They left everything else locked in the damaged car, figuring they'd come back for it later.

Elijah sat next to Marco, holding his duffel bag between his knees. He unzipped it, took out the Manila envelope full of documents, and showed it to Marco. "I found this, by the way. Nice hiding place. Unless we get burgled. Thieves will go straight for the gaming stuff, man."

Marco stared blankly at the envelope. After a few seconds Elijah put it away again. He rubbed Serafina's ears and tried to think of something else to say.

"So, I figure we can go to the county fairgrounds," he said. "I mean, after we get checked out. I doubt we're in bad enough shape to score a room in the ER for the night. And there's an evacuation center set up at the fairgrounds."

"My daughter can give you a ride there, once she gets into town," offered Mrs. Lucas. "I'd ask you to stay with us at her place, but she barely has enough room to squeeze me in, let alone two strapping young men and a dog. She'd be happy to offer you a lift, though. And she could swing back to your car first so you can get the rest of your things."

"That would be great, Mrs. Lucas," said Elijah.

"Yeah," echoed Marco in a quiet, vague voice. "Yeah, that sounds good."

More silence.

Marco cleared his throat. Then cleared it again. "Hey, man. Listen. I, uh . . . I'm glad you saved those documents."

"Anytime." Elijah paused. "Well—I *hope* I never have to do it again. But you know what I mean."

"Sure, man. And, uh . . . You did a good job today. I'm proud of you."

"Thanks, Uncle Marco."

"Dude, don't call me that. It's weird."

"I know, right? So—does this mean I'm not grounded anymore?"

"Don't push your luck."

Marco patted Elijah on the shoulder. Not gently, because Marco wasn't that kind of guy.

18

Brenna

On the way to the hospital, Nicole fell asleep. Brenna couldn't blame her. This had been a completely exhausting morning.

Keegan sat beside Brenna, wrapped in a blanket, still damp from the lake. He'd been unusually quiet since boarding the helicopter, but now he spoke up.

"So, Brenna. I . . . I'm really sorry for the way I acted this weekend. The way I kept acting like I didn't think you knew what you were talking about. I guess I just . . . I wanted to feel like I could be useful. Like I wasn't just tagging along, being clueless. I knew you would've rather had Elijah there than me. I guess I wanted to prove that I could hold my own."

Brenna sighed. "You didn't have to prove anything to me. And I really wish you hadn't acted like *I* had to prove something to *you*."

"I shouldn't have. I'm sorry." He looked as if he wanted to ask her something else but wasn't sure how.

"Well, I appreciate that. And I'm glad we all made it out without worse injuries."

She was glad he didn't ask if they were still friends. She wasn't sure how she'd answer that. But what mattered right now was that all three of them were okay. If Keegan hadn't pulled Nicole away from Brenna and sprinted for the lake, they might not have made it. Or if Nicole hadn't gotten that tree off Brenna's leg—or if Keegan hadn't packed a mini-shovel—or if Nicole hadn't salvaged Brenna's compass. In the end, none of them could've survived without the others.

***

Nicole sat with Brenna at the hospital while they waited for their families to arrive.

"My parents told me all of Hayden got evacuated," said Nicole. Brenna nodded. Her mom had said the same thing when Brenna had called her. She'd been limited to a short call on an ancient hospital payphone, since her cell phone hadn't emerged from Nicole's backpack in working order. Nicole—back to her usual optimistic self—had suggested packing their phones in rice to dry them out. But Brenna suspected the heat had fried them even if the plunge in the lake hadn't short-circuited them. Of course, the loss of a cell phone wouldn't seem like much compared to the loss of her whole home. But it was hard to even wrap her mind around what *that* could mean.

"We'll have to stay with my aunt until we know if our place survived," Nicole went on.

"I don't know where we'll stay," Brenna murmured, only half focused. "We don't have any family close by. And all our friends live in Hayden."

"You'll figure something out."

"Yeah. My mom didn't seem too worried about that. She was mostly freaked out that she hadn't heard from me all morning. And that I almost died in a wildfire."

"That does tend to freak parents out. Man, the next time we go camping, I swear I won't complain at all."

Brenna smiled. "You actually want to go camping again after this?"

"I mean, anything's got to be easier and more fun than facing a wall of flames. Right?"

"Probably," Brenna agreed.

Elijah

The county fairgrounds had become a massive campsite. Tents, trailers, and cars clustered together, filling all the available space. No matter where Elijah stood, there wasn't enough open space for him to stretch out both arms. He wove his way through the pop-up city, holding Serafina's leash with one hand and his phone with the other. It was almost sunset. Instead of an angry, glowing orange, the light was a soft, natural gold. But Elijah could still smell smoke. He'd probably be smelling it for days.

"How far from the main entrance are you?" he said into his phone.

Brenna, who'd hijacked her mom's phone to call him, answered, "About eight rows back, and five rows from the far south end."

"GPS coordinates, please?"

"Oh, shut up!" She laughed. "I'm standing in front of my mom's RV."

Elijah sidestepped a group of little kids playing tag. He zigzagged between tents, around vehicles. People were crying, laughing, gossiping, passing food around. Serafina trotted beside him—unfazed by everything, as usual.

Was that Brenna's mom's RV, about a hundred feet ahead? Why did all recreational vehicles look so much alike?

"Are you wearing a blue bandanna?" Elijah asked through the phone.

"Yep. And I've got a glorious white cast on my leg. The crutches might be another giveaway."

"I think I see you. I'm waving . . . "

"I see you!" Brenna shouted into the phone. Elijah saw her arm shoot into the air. He jogged toward her, Serafina trotting at his heels.

Seconds later, Brenna dropped her crutches so she could wrap her arms around him. Elijah picked them up for her after a moment. "Since when does Serafina *like* you?" Brenna demanded, nodding at the dog.

"Since I saved her from a wildfire, obviously. Are you okay?"

"Overall, I'm amazingly okay." She tucked her crutch under her armpit again. "I mean, there's the broken leg, obviously. And a little shortness of breath, still, from the smoke inhalation, but the doctor gave me meds for that. Oh, and my back and legs are covered in first-degree burns, but those should heal in a week or two if I use the ointment they gave me . . ."

Elijah shook his head. "You have a really low bar for 'okay.'"

Brenna laughed and shrugged. "Well, it could've been so much worse."

"I know what you mean," said Elijah, remembering the unbearable heat of the car.

"And what about you—are you okay?"

"Clean bill of health. Marco's car is trashed, but it already had one foot in the grave anyway. We managed to salvage all the stuff we had in the trunk. Just wish I knew if our house made it."

He knew the odds weren't good. But then again, what were the odds that he and Brenna—and Keegan and Nicole and Mrs. Lucas and even Serafina—would have survived a fire this deadly?

Brenna nodded and glanced toward the RV. "I don't think my mom has even processed that we might lose everything. She's too relieved that I'm in one piece—mostly, at least. But I heard that the fire's almost fifty percent contained now. It should be fully under control in the next couple days. By then we'll know how badly our neighborhoods are damaged."

Using her crutches, Brenna hopped around to the back of her mom's RV and perched on the back bumper. Elijah joined her, leaning against the back of the vehicle. Serafina flopped on the grass.

"I can't stop thinking about how much it took for Marco to build that house," said Elijah quietly. "All those years of working and saving. And all the effort and money and time to get it built. I know this kind of thing happens every day. You hear about it happening to other people—on the news and stuff. And those people always say, 'We can rebuild.' But—what if we can't? Rebuilding costs a lot of money. What if we can't manage it?"

"You'll find a way."

"See, people always say that too. But what if they only say it because there's nothing else to say? What if they're just fooling themselves?"

"Elijah, we all just survived a raging forest fire. If we can do that, we can do anything. Especially if we all support each other." Brenna looked down at the cast on her leg. "So no, I can't *guarantee* that everything's going to be okay. I'm not sure of it. But I can still *believe* it."

Elijah smiled. "Yeah. I mean, if I can get this dog on my side, anything's possible."

He looked at the sunset and took a deep, steadying breath. This time the smoke didn't bother him quite so much.

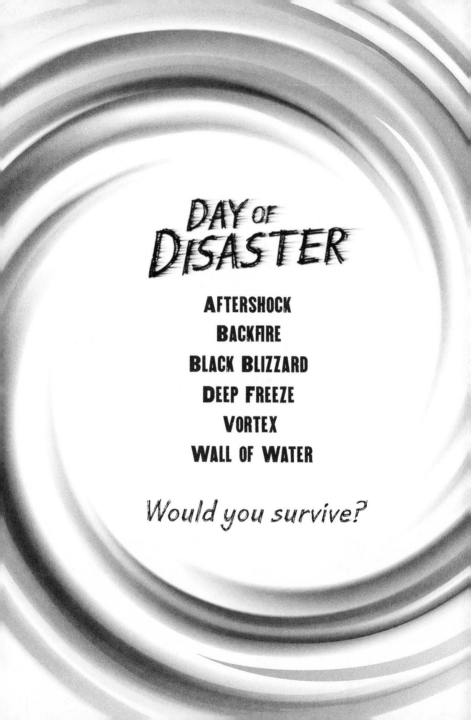

DAY OF DISASTER

Would you survive?

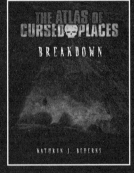
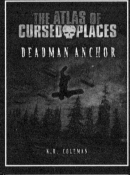

About the Author

Vanessa Acton is a writer and editor based in Minneapolis, Minnesota. She enjoys stalking dead people (also known as historical research), drinking too much tea, and taking long walks during her home state's annual three-week thaw.